The Emerald Curse

Uncovering the Family Legacy

The Emerald Curse
Uncovering the Family Legacy

A Cristiane Bradford Novelette

Sirrah Medeiros

Tundra Swan Press
Virginia

TUNDRA SWAN PRESS, October 2021

Copyright ©2010, 2021 by Sirrah Medeiros

All rights reserved. This story or any portion thereof may not be reproduced or used in any manner whatsoever without the express written permission of the publisher except for the use of brief quotations in a book review.

This expanded and revised version of The Emerald Curse is published in the United States of America by Tundra Swan Press and originally appeared as an award-winning short story in Vicious Spirits, A Ghostly Compendium by Members of the Key Publications Network.

The events depicted in this story are entirely fictitious. Any references to historical events, real people, or real places are used fictitiously. Other names, characters, places, and events are products of the author's imagination.

Library of Congress Control Number (LCCN): 2021921155

ISBN: 979-8-9852025-0-2

Friday Night

"Ah, my hand! My hand! Help me!" David screamed in agony, then immediately followed with a full belly laugh. "Ha-ha, gotcha!" Turning to his friends with his arm still pressed deep into the crevasse, he saw his attempt at humor hit flat. The others rolled their eyes and shook their heads at him. "Oh, fine. Can't take a tiny joke, huh?" He turned back to the task, feeling around in the darkness.

David hauled a medallion from the broken sarcophagus and brought it up to the moonlight. The deep emerald jewels refracted the light, sending beams of soft iridescence throughout the crypt. The shimmer cast an eerie glow in the room, revealing the dust-covered contents of the small chamber. Three of them moved closer to inspect.

"What is it?" Robby tried to pull the object from David's grasp. David clung to the green jewel, not willing to give it up to the others for inspection.

"Nothing. It's a piece of stained glass from the broken window," David dashed the trinket out of the light. He passed a hurried look toward Cristiane, gave a slight wink, and pocketed the necklace into his jacket. His companions dismissed the finding and looked around the small, grubby building as David turned on a flashlight, drawing the others' attention to their surroundings.

It was four days before All Hallows' Eve—Friday night—and the teens rummaged through the old cemetery. Some tombstones were so old they were crumbling and difficult to read. The carved stones were no match for the elements and the lack of maintenance over the centuries. Much of the cemetery required repair. Weeds and tall grass took over many of the plot markers. Only the loftier, more lavish stones were easy to find in the damp, over-grown resting place of ancestors long forgotten by their descendants. The legends fascinated the teens. And since they started high school, they visited the old churchyard every year around Halloween.

This was their fourth visit; as seniors, they stayed in the graveyard overnight as a last hurrah. This time next year, they would be at college. They would only think of this place as they told ghost stories at a frat house Halloween party. They wanted this last time walking among the deceased to be special. A last *dance with the dead*. So, they wanted to explore everything. During other visits, they hadn't ventured into a crypt. But this time, David couldn't pass up the opportunity to venture inside. The boards over the broken window called to him like an open invitation to peer inside. He tore off the boards before anyone could voice a protest. As any teens would do, Cristiane, Robby, and Tina followed David through the window.

"Hey, look at this." Tina dusted the top of an etched plaque that stood in front of heavy, towering doors. The other three came around to Tina. Robby brought up a flashlight so they could read the inscription.

The Madison Family Women

Rachel resides in the center of this crypt.
Recognized by her daughter, Constance Madison Worthington,
Contributor to North Andover Society and the town's development.
Rachel's mother and aunt were accused of witchcraft and then killed
by the North Andover townspeople
during the Salem Witchcraft Trials.

Their remains are encased in the crypt vault.
Carolyn Madison Brown 1654-1692
Prudence Madison 1651-1694
Rachel Madison 1676-1734

"What the hell?" Cristiane stumbled as she stepped back from the others. The inscription shook her. David started laughing and looked at his girlfriend with a playful look.

"What's the big deal, Cris? We've talked about this stuff before. They took some people from Andover to Salem for trial. The townspeople even hung some of them, from what my grandpa used to say. Everyone knows this ugly history, but no one talks about it. It's no surprise a few were taken care of right here in town." He tried to pull her close as he approached, but she brushed him off.

"I know, but I think those last names are in my family tree. I don't want to be related to these people." Irritated with David, she pushed him away and walked over to Tina and Robby. "Let's go. This place is giving me the creeps."

"Isn't Worthington your mom's maiden name?" Unfazed by Cristiane, David sauntered behind the group.

"Yes, but Madison is in our family tree, too. Leave it alone. I want to get out of here." Cristiane was anxious to leave and waved a dismissive hand toward David.

Tina and Robby followed Cristiane back through the broken window, shimmying themselves over the windowsill with little grace. David came through last. He wrestled with the boards to cover the window opening, but they wouldn't stay. He shrugged his shoulders, leaving the area open, and moved to join the others.

"So, that was cool. Cris, you never mentioned that your family dated back to the witch trials."

Tina and Robby nodded in agreement and waited for their friend to respond, but Cristiane wasn't happy. She stood in place, brooding over the inscription. The others tried to get her to move. But realizing she would not budge, they started pulling out sleeping bags from their packs and arranged them on the ground. Robby nudged Cristiane once they set everything up and, with a sweep of his hand, pointed her gaze toward the makeshift camp. "We should camp here for the night. We got it all set up, Cris. Relax and get your mind off that stuff inside. I'm sure you're not related to them. Your family would've told you by now."

"Yeah. Yeah, I guess you're right. Thanks, Robby." Cristiane looked at him and gave a weak smile. Then she shook her arms as if to rid herself of the thoughts. As she looked around, she saw David had set up the gas stove. "Oh, great! Let me get the stuff for s'mores from my bag."

Tina let out a deep breath and plopped herself down next to Cristiane. "Perfect!"

The foursome sat around their makeshift campfire, sharing treats and telling old ghost stories. A brief time later, the conversation changed to the future. They talked about what schools they applied to for college, what each would major in, and if they could get into their top-choice schools. Suddenly, a loud beeping sounded, and the girls screamed.

David roared with laughter as he dug out a cell phone from his back pocket. "Sorry, ladies. I forgot I set my alarm." He hit a button, and the noise stopped abruptly.

"You're gonna get us caught, David Ryan." Cristiane smacked his arm with the back of her hand. She shook her head and then laughed with her friends.

"Well, excuse me for wanting to wish my girlfriend a happy birthday at the exact moment she turns 18." David grabbed her in his arms. "Happy birthday, Cristiane." He pulled her close and planted a firm kiss on her lips in front of the others.

Blushing, Cristiane pulled back, "Well, I guess you're forgiven then." She ran her hands through her hair, regaining some of her composure from the alarm and David's kiss. Tina and Robby uttered their birthday wishes while David pulled out a bottle of champagne. While popping the cork, David didn't hold on to it. The cork flew into the crypt's open window, making another loud noise as it slammed against the opposing interior wall. Cristiane gave him a glaring look as he poured champagne into four plastic cups.

"Cheers, Cris. You're now an adult and can do whatever you want." David raised his glass and flashed a smile over the rim at Cristiane. She knew what he wanted, but they hadn't been together before. Cristiane wasn't ready for a commitment or to get physical with David. She returned a brief smile and sipped her drink.

Suddenly, an icy burst of wind shot through the group, extinguished the fire, and left them in bitter darkness. Tina choked on her champagne and coughed violently as the others tried to make sense of what had happened. Robby walked over, pulling Tina close to comfort her. She tried several times to clear her throat so she could breathe. Cristiane started sobbing and quietly muttering as she pointed toward the back of the Madison crypt.

"Wha—wha—what is that?" She shivered from the icy chill. She cried and pointed toward the back of the small building. However, as the others regained their composure from the cold and turned in the direction where she pointed, whatever she saw vanished.

"What are you talking about, Cris? There's nothing there." David came up and put his arms around her, rubbing her back to provide some sense of security. "My god, Cris. You're freezing. Come on. Let's call it a night and get some sleep."

Cristiane nervous, nodded her head, snuggling closer to David as he guided her toward her sleeping bag. The evening was unusual, warm for late October in New Hampshire. The mild weather was one reason the foursome decided to camp in the open air. However, although the icy chill was gone as quickly as it arrived, Cristiane lay nestled in her bag, shivering. David watched over her; concern set across his brow. But he said nothing, in fear of spooking her even more.

He inched over a bit and sat on his sleeping bag. Tina and Robby set up a short distance away and were settled in their spots, quietly chatting. David grabbed another champagne bottle, opened it in silence, raised it to his lips, and took a long draw. He pulled the emerald pendant from his pocket and turned it over and over in his hand. It was amazing, well-crafted and an heirloom. The emeralds were cut to fit into an odd triangle shape, surrounded by an intricate silver design. He looked over at Cristiane; she was asleep already. He held the jewel up toward his girlfriend and smiled.

Saturday Afternoon

David stood at Cristiane's front door and rang the bell. He was a bit dehydrated from the second bottle of champagne, but otherwise felt fine. It was early afternoon, so he had some time to clear his head earlier in the day before seeing Cristiane. He was antsy and jumped when her father opened the door.

"Oh! Hi, Mr. Bradford. Is Cris around? I wanted to surprise her with a present before the party tonight."

Cristiane's dad, Jeffrey, wasn't too keen on David, but most fathers of teen daughters are a bit protective. "Yeah, she's here. Thought you two were fighting the way she was behaving this morning after your camp out in the cemetery." Jeffrey straightened, standing to his full height of six-four. "You hurt her son, and you're gonna have to answer to me."

David edged past Mr. Bradford. "Umm, wouldn't dream of hurting Cristiane, sir. I don't know what's wrong. I bet she's tired, that's all."

"Better be all that's wrong, David. Go on and give her your gift." Done interrogating his daughter's boyfriend, Mr. Bradford closed the door and walked away. David uttered a sigh of relief and bounded up the stairs to Cristiane's room, smiling at the thought of her reaction to his gift.

Cristiane heard a couple of quick raps on her open bedroom door as David walked right in while she turned from her desk. "David! What are you doing here?" She got up and gave him a quick hug and kiss, peeking toward the door to make sure one of her parents wasn't standing nearby.

"I know we would not get together until the party tonight, but I wanted to give you something." He pulled a small gift box from his jacket and handed it to Cristiane. He smiled and watched as she turned the box over in her hands. "I thought you might want to wear it tonight."

"What is it?" Unable to contain her curiosity, she ripped the ribbon and paper from the box and pulled the lid off, tossing it on her bed. She gasped as she pulled the pendant from the tissue paper. "David, it's beautiful, but too expensive. I can't accept something like this; it's too much!"

"Yes, you can, and you will." David took it from her and undid the clasp to help her put on the necklace. "When I looked at it, I knew you had to have it. Don't worry about the cost. I didn't even pay anything for it."

"What?" Cristiane shot David a quizzical look before turning to look at the necklace in the mirror. It was beautiful with the emeralds catching the light. It was an unusual design. "You didn't steal it, did you?"

"Well... if you're being technical, then yes." David shrugged as he sat on the edge of her bed. "No one is going to miss it. I pulled the necklace out of the coffin. I cleaned it up this morning when I got home. Isn't it beautiful? And on you, it seems perfect."

Cristiane crinkled up her brow and reached to undo the clasp at the back of her neck. "Oh, no. I can't keep this. It must go back, David." Her hands were shaking while she tried to get the clasp to come apart. "Last night was too creepy. I don't want to wear it."

David took her hands, pulling her to him; he kissed her to stop her protests. "Babe, it's okay. Nothing happened last night; it was only our imaginations going wild in the dark. The necklace is stunning—like it was meant for you. It even highlights your gorgeous green eyes."

Cristiane softened, not wanting to hurt his feelings. "Oh, all right. It is beautiful, isn't it?" She caressed it with her fingertips.

David kissed her again. A shock made him jerk back from her. "Wow, what was that?"

Cristiane glared at him. "What are you talking about?"

He put his hand to his mouth. "That shock, didn't you feel it? It was the strongest static shock I've ever felt. My lip is still tingling."

"You're crazy. It must be the effects of drinking all that champagne."

"Maybe. I guess I better go, anyway. I'll come by a little before seven to pick you up, then we can get Robby and Tina. Wear the necklace. It'll look killer with your costume." David gave her a quick kiss, jumping again as he received another shock. He shook his head and waved bye, heading out the door.

Saturday Night

Shortly after six, Cristiane stood in front of her full-length mirror, checking her costume one last time. She was supposed to be a witch, but all she wore was a slim-fitting long black dress with a deep collar that showed off the necklace. David was right. It appeared that the necklace was designed for her, and her green eyes sparkled all the brighter with the haunting emerald stones at her neck. Her hair was long and dark. She teased, crunched, and sprayed it so it looked wicked and sinful with her makeup.

Her father would blow a gasket if he saw her dressed like this. Thankful for their plans, he was gone with Mom for a date night.

Her cell phone rang.

"Hello?"

"Cris, it's David. I can't pick you up for the dance. I just got in the room and found my cell phone to call you." His speech trembled through the phone. Cristiane heard weariness in his voice, but thought nothing of it.

"What are you talking about? Get over here. We have a party to attend. You shouldn't have had champagne last night." She was irritated with him. David hated parties, and she had to talk him into going to Michelle's Halloween bash in the first place.

"It's not that. I—I'm in the hospital. I got—"

"What?" Cristiane screamed before realizing it. She looked toward her door, then remembered her parents were gone. "Sorry, I didn't mean to do that. I'm coming right over!"

"No, don't do that. Just go—" David looked at the handset, realizing he heard the phone click off. She had hung up on him.

Twenty minutes later, Cristiane was by his side in the hospital room, still dressed in her costume for the party. She held his hand while looking over his bandages and the cast on his left leg. They had wrapped his head with heavy gauze, as were his right shoulder and left arm. Her hand was shaking as she cradled his hand and kissed an unwrapped spot on his forehead.

"It was the weirdest thing, Cris. It wasn't because of last night, I felt fine. I didn't drink that much." He made sure no one could hear him. "Remember that burst of cold last night? Well, I felt that inside my car right before the accident, and I had the windows up because it was cool today. Right?" He looked at her with a sheepish stare. "And... well, I felt someone in the car with me, too. I know. I know. It's weird."

Cristiane was giving him the funniest look that made David think he had imagined the whole thing.

"That's impossible, David." Cristiane was trying to remain calm, but her own vision from the night before flashed through her mind. She didn't want to think about it.

"I know. You're right. I'm remembering it wrong. The doc said I have a slight concussion, so I'm not thinking straight. They want to keep me overnight for observation." David felt better. He was certain the incident was an accident. Not giving it any more thought, he smiled at Cristiane. "You go. Go to the party so everyone can see how great you are."

"I don't want to go without you, David." Cristiane shook her head.

"Please, go for me. I don't want to feel guilty about ruining the evening for both of us. It's your birthday. Go have a fun time."

"Oh, all right. Only because I still haven't called Robby or Tina. I bet they're wondering why we haven't been by to pick them up yet."

Cristiane stood up and smoothed out her dress. David admired her figure when he felt a sudden pain in his stomach, like someone had hit him. He winced slightly.

"Don't worry about them. I called Robby while you were driving over here. They're already at the party waiting for you. Don't freak them out by not showing up." David reached to take her hand. As they touched, he felt another pain. David kissed her and let go of her hand quickly, too. As soon as he stopped touching Cristiane, the pain was gone.

Reluctant, Cristiane lumbered to the door, stopping in the entryway. "Promise me you'll get some rest. Don't let any of the guys hound you." Turning for a last glance at David, she blew him a kiss before walking around the corner.

Saturday Night - Late

A few hours later, Cristiane found herself alone at Michelle's house. Without David by her side, she felt strange. Her costume was incredible, but it was too revealing for her to be alone at the party. Some guys came to see if she and David had broken up. When she told them of his accident and that he was in the hospital, they hurried on. Of course, they didn't leave without first looking her over from head to toe, like a piece of prized meat.

She sensed she was on display and was about to look for Tina and Robby to tell them she was leaving when Jack came up to her. He smelled of beer and stood too close, looking down her dress as he talked to her.

"Cristiane, you look—delicious. I hear you're alone tonight." He spoke with confidence. Jack was the running back for the football team. Someone rumored him to have a scholarship, and the season wasn't over. A typical jock, making his rounds through several girls each year. He was tall, muscular, attractive—and he knew it. Cristiane had a crush on him early last year, which Tina had made the mistake of gossiping around the school. Too bad his personality was horrendous.

However, Cristiane wasn't in the mood for him or his flirting. "Jack, stop. David is in the hospital. We didn't break up or anything." She stepped back a few paces, but Jack followed her.

"I heard. What a shame, and to waste such a night with the birthday girl when you are dressed so sweetly." He grabbed Cristiane's waist and pulled her close while he guided her to the crowd dancing nearby. "Relax and enjoy your night. I can give you an evening to remember."

Jack bent down to kiss her neck. She tried to push him away, which only made him pull her closer. To anyone watching, it would appear they were making out on the dance floor. His hands were around her, wrapped across her back. He was so massive that it was difficult for her to get out of his grasp. Cristiane realized she was terrified as she spit in his ear, "Jack, let go of me, or I'm going to make a scene."

Jack wouldn't stop. He groped at her and nuzzled into her neck as Cristiane pushed to get away. She heard a grumble near her neck. "No way!" A split second later, he jumped away from her. "What the hell was that?" He touched his shoulder, a fresh burn mark on his shirt.

"Leave me alone, Jack." Cristiane didn't care what he was talking about; she wanted to get away quickly.

Shaken, she snatched a soda off the table and walked back to the pool, away from the crowd. A moment later, Jack walked out with a beer in hand, raised it toward Cristiane slightly, and kept walking. She noticed the triangle-shaped burn on his shirt. It wasn't there earlier when he came up to her.

At least he got the message. She watched Jack as he strutted, confident around the pool. He was looking at the girls, seeking his next conquest. As she regarded Jack, she felt a freezing blast of air, like the night before. She peered around. No one else seemed to notice. Then she looked toward Jack. There was an odd fog behind him. Jack also seemed to have felt the icy chill. She noticed he stopped walking and shook as if cold. A sinking feeling grabbed at the pit of her stomach as the form took shape.

Cristiane stood mesmerized, watching as the shape of a woman formed behind Jack. Long, billowing hair and gown trailed the misty apparition. The phantom appeared to look at Cristiane for a moment before raising her arms toward Jack. Cristiane dropped her soda and screamed as the apparition latched onto Jack and pulled him into the pool.

Everyone glared at Cristiane, and then they heard the splash, turning to see Jack flailing in the pool. A roar of laughter broke out as the crowd watched Jack bobble up and down in the water. Only when he was having trouble did the crowd quiet down. He knew how to swim. He had been on the county swim team for years before football took over his athletic career. Some kids thought he was goofing around.

People murmured as they watched; a group of guys joking, teased Jack as he fought to stay above the waterline. Cristiane stayed back and watched. She could see something under Jack holding onto his legs, keeping him from getting to the stairs. She soon realized that none of the others saw the apparition. Knowing that he wouldn't win against whatever was holding him, Cristiane looked around, trying to decide how to help.

Another form caught Cristiane's eye. This was a different apparition, more defined than the previous in her appearance. She was beautiful and thin, a wisp of an image in the evening air as she glided to Cristiane's side. With a tilt of her head, she looked at Cristiane with curiosity. She pointed toward the emerald pendant around Cristiane's neck.

Cristiane shook with fear and reached up, grazed the pendant, and felt a warmth to the touch. A fleeting glance of understanding crossed Cristiane's eyes as she veered her eyes toward Jack. *Did the pendant burn that mark into his shirt?*

The ghost acknowledged her newfound understanding with a nod and a soft utterance as she pointed to the necklace, "Cursed." The figure darted over to the pool. With a last glance at Cristiane, it then swooped into the pool and extracted the other phantom holding Jack down in the water. Both figures vanished through the privacy wall.

Robby and Tina showed up from their make-out session to see what was causing the commotion. As they came to Cristiane's side, Robby looked at her with a knowing gaze. He asked her in front of Tina, "Are you okay?" Then, closer with his voice low as Tina watched the crowd around Jack. "I saw them too, but don't mention it to Tina. She doesn't believe me."

Shock rocked Cristiane as Robby confirmed what she saw. She latched onto the back of a nearby chair and closed her eyes. After a few deep breaths, she was calmer but still afraid to look around.

"I'm gonna head home. This has gotten way out of hand. I want out of here before Jack makes a federal case out of his dump in the pool and swooning for attention from the ladies."

"Sounds like a clever idea," Tina responded. She wrapped her arm around Robby's waist. They walked together toward the open doorway. "Text when you get home, so we know you're okay."

"Sure, no problem. See you later." Cristiane walked through the house and went straight to her car. She waited until Robby and Tina climbed into his car and followed them to her road. As she turned down her street to head home, she flicked her headlights to signal a goodbye.

Midnight

Unable to remove the necklace, Cristiane braided her hair before going to bed, so it wouldn't get tangled in the chain while she slept. Her parents weren't due home for another hour. She felt scared and alone as she plumped up several pillows, building a cocoon of comfort around herself. With the blanket up pulled up close under her chin, she tossed and turned for quite some time until she settled down.

She turned on her side and startled at the hardness against her hip. Cristiane sat up and found herself in a cramped, dark room with several others lying on the floor and sitting against the walls, many sleeping. As her eyes adjusted to the darkness, she heard a man moaning to her left, a few feet away. The smell of dirt, sweat, and human excrement caught her off-guard. Cristiane covered her mouth and nose with her hands. *Disgusting. What is this?*

The nearby cries of women whom she could not see frightened her. "Who's there?" Cristiane called out through the darkness. Her heart raced, and her breathing quickened out of fear. "Where am I?" She put her hand out to her side, feeling about, trying to make sense of her surroundings. Touching someone, she gasped. "Oh, I'm sorry… Who? What is this?"

"Hello?" a youthful voice called out.

"Hello? Yes, I'm Cristiane. What is your name? Where are we?"

"You don't know where you are? I'm Dorothy." The young girl spoke through the crowded room. "You're in jail, silly." Dorothy moved closer to Cristiane.

"Jail? What could you have done to land in jail?" It dismayed Cristiane, the madness of sending such a young girl to jail, exposing her to such filth. She could see an outline of a small child because of the first slivers of morning light drifting in through a small window high on the wall.

"I'm not sure. The judge talked with me yesterday. He called me a witch. A couple of our neighbors were there too. They said I bit them over and over, which is not funny to say I did it. I know it was Max, but none of them believed me." Dorothy stated matter of fact, without concern for her surroundings or the stench that drifted through the cramped quarters.

"Who is Max?"

"Oh, Maximillian. He's my pet snake. The judge called him a family, some witch pet, but he's only a snake." A calm Dorothy played with a string dangling from her dress hem.

"Do you mean a familiar?"

"Yes, that's what he said," Dorothy nodded as she jumped in her seat, happy to hear the right word. "I don't know what that means, but I've heard the word used a lot with so many people being called witches and thrown in jail. I don't understand, but the guards have been nice to me."

They both remained quiet for a few minutes. The cries of the women nearby churning dread in Cristiane's mind as she listened to Dorothy. "I'm glad they're treating you well. How long have you been here?" Cristiane peeked around the room. The morning light came in brighter, shedding a fresh look at the dreadful scene before her.

All the people were dressed in old, tattered, and torn clothing. Dirt and grime, interlaced with the stench of dried blood and urine. Cristiane noticed that all had some form of injury—bruises, lacerations, and broken bones. A horrifying mangle of depravity. Two buckets, one at each far corner of the room. She wondered what the buckets were for until she saw a man standing in front of one and relieve himself in front of everyone. Cristiane choked down the vomit that threatened to erupt.

"A few days, maybe a week. It's hard to tell." Dorothy worried her lip as she worked her memory. "The old man was put in the town square two days ago, so I think it's been a week."

"What happened to the—" The guard cut Cristiane off.

"Line up in rows. Get up and get moving. Come on now!" A large, hulky man bellowed as he came around the corner, followed by several more guards. Chains and locks overloaded in their arms. The people surrounding her groaned and shuffled as they stood up. Several moved into position, while others followed behind them. Cristiane counted 20 people. She and Dorothy lined up beside each other at the back.

"Old Mr. Corey. You'll see soon enough." Sadness laced Dorothy's words, as they were barely an audible whisper.

Cristiane's eyes bulged as she watched the guards pull and kick the sickly people in front of her, each person shackled to the other. Their feet buckled with metal brackets and a heavy chain-linked one prisoner to the next. Cristiane began to hyperventilate as she realized she would also be cuffed and chained like the others. Tears spilled over the brim of her eyes.

Dorothy grabbed Cristiane's hand and squeezed. "It's okay. They won't hurt you right away. Stay quiet and do what the guards say."

Cristiane couldn't speak. She nodded and gave the young girl a weak smile.

"Dorothy, stop touching the inmate!" The head guard roared as he kneeled to cuff Cristiane's legs with chains.

"Yes, Mr. Charles. Sorry." Dorothy displayed no hint of fear. She smiled at him and offered her hands out, waiting for the chains.

He tapped her hands down and laughed. "Don't be silly, child. You know the chains won't fit you. Stay with the group, as always." His demeanor flipped from a rough, burly guard to that of a sweet, fatherly figure. He squatted down to be eye-to-eye with Dorothy. As he wiped the dirt from under her eyes and smoothed out her hair, his face softened. A deep sigh escaped him, and he put his hands on her shoulders. "You may stay near your new friend, but don't misbehave. If I heard the magistrate correctly, they're going to let you go home today."

"Really?" Dorothy sounded relieved as she grasped a handful of material from Cristiane's dress. "I'll behave. I promise."

Charles leaned in close to Cristiane. "Do nothing stupid, witch. Watch the others, do as you're told, and the guards will leave you alone. If you hurt Dorothy, I will burn you alive myself. Shield her eyes as much as possible from what you're about to witness." Cristiane nodded as the tears again began rolling down her cheeks. "Good."

He moved back and gave Dorothy a huge smile and pat on the back before marching out the door.

As the group shuffled through the prison, Cristiane pondered over her predicament. Her eyes downcast, she lumbered behind, deep in thought as the group entered the open air. After passing a building as they hobbled down the street, she realized she was watching blood drops fall to the ground every few feet. Cristiane peered around the prisoner in front of her while she followed the blood trail. It led to the first prisoner in her line—to a gaping wound. Broken bone protruded below the elbow, skin tore open, and flesh dangled an inch from an old woman's bruised and battered arm—the source of the blood drips. Flies came and went from the wound, nipping and biting at the tasty treat. The old woman hunched over and swatting at the flies when not cradling the arm close to her body. The guards didn't bother to bind her hands, unlike Cristiane and the other prisoners. Little good it did her. The old woman had no use of her arm—torn, bloodied, and mangled, as it was. Horrified, Cristiane stared at the wound until the group stopped, and she bumped into the person chained to her.

"Don't plant yourselves. Fan out and give witness, so you may learn and confess your sins." A man dressed in a dusty black suit yelled from a tall, make-shift podium. "Repent witches, and you may save yourselves from the punishment you now see with your eyes."

Guards shoved the line leaders with the butt of their weapons together. The guards pushed and positioned the next in line where they wanted the prisoners to stand and then forced the following prisoners to shuffle up and out.

Cristiane, being at the back of the group, turned away from the town center. She followed the person whom they chained her to and shuffled to the edge of the podium. She had little room to fan out and squeezed in between the prisoner and the podium stairs to her right and then faced the town center. Dorothy pressed between Cristiane and the prisoner to her left, holding tight to Cristiane's dress.

As Cristiane's eyes adapted to the bright morning sun, she noticed a large mound of boulders on a wagon bed and nothing more. The prisoner group gathered around in a wide-sweeping circle facing the boulders. Soon, the smell of rotting flesh and urine brushed about by the breeze in her direction. She choked back the bile that rose in the back of her throat. The stench overwhelmed her senses. She squinted while lifting her bound hands to block the sun. What lay before her was beyond comprehension.

Who could do such a thing to another human being? She pondered as tears streaked down her face. Underneath the pile of boulders was an elderly man. At least, that's what he looked like to Cristiane. Sparse gray hair on his head and a thick gray beard, covered with trails of dried blood. The bald spot on the top of his head had a seeping gash where flies swarmed to feed. His arms, bloodied and bruised, were partially visible under the heap of rock pressing on his chest. His feet were swollen and covered in sores, the only part of his body visible, other than the poor man's arms and head. *I hope he's dead, for his own sake.* Cristiane prayed as she took in the scene before her.

Dorothy tugged at Cristiane's dress as she motioned with her head toward the tortured man and muttered. "See, Mr. Corey."

Dorothy glanced up and noticed Cristiane's terrified expression as the tears pouring down her cheeks. "It's terribly sad, isn't it? I don't know what he did. He's refused to speak, and each day the guards are ordered to place more boulders on him. He was always nice to me, but the judge says Mr. Corey is a witch." Dorothy lifted her hand and pointed a tiny index finger at the man in the suit. She then dropped it so the guards would not catch her.

"Witch or not, this is beyond cruel." Cristiane choked out in reply before wailing into a fit of despair.

"Quiet. They'll get angry if you make noise. Please, stop crying." Dorothy patted Cristiane's dress.

Cristiane slowly blew out a ragged breath while attempting to control her emotions. As she quieted down, she noticed no one made a sound. The prisoners, the guards, the resident onlookers near the surrounding buildings—all were silent as she wiped at her face with the back of her bound hands.

"Carolyn, are you ready to confess your sins?" The judge hissed from behind her, so close she could feel his breath through her hair. "Perhaps you can persuade Giles and his wife over there to confess." The judge waved toward the older woman who had led the prisoners to the town center. The woman's blood trail that mesmerized Cristiane on the march now dripped into a puddle at Mrs. Corey's bare feet.

Cristiane didn't respond. Instead, she quieted down until his laughter subsided, and he walked back up the steps of the podium. Cristiane's eyes lingered at Mrs. Corey's blood puddle and then traveled up the old woman's body, meeting her gaze. The old woman returned an understanding nod but said nothing. Her eyes reflecting the no-win situation they found themselves in. Nothing any of them did, confess or not, would change the judge's mind or the minds of the townspeople looking to feed their blood lust.

Cristiane continued to look at each prisoner. They ranged in age and gender; all were tired and forlorn. Dorothy being the youngest and only child, no more than five from Cristiane's observation. *What monster imprisons such a young girl? It is absurd.* Cristiane mused. Dorothy kept her innocence, in part because the guards did not treat her like the other inmates. Her fellow prisoners looked hollowed-out, existing, waiting for their sentences to be carried out. Guilt or innocence didn't matter, their fates were written on their faces, void of hope.

"Men, has the prisoner confessed?" The judge yelled to the two guards nearest Mr. Corey's head.

"No, Your Honor. Not a word." One yelled back in reply.

"Mrs. Corey, last chance to persuade your husband to enter a plea. Cat got his tongue. He can speak. We all know him. He isn't mute." The judge chided, as Mrs. Corey looked back at him with pure hatred.

"So be it." The judge turned his gaze back to the guards. "Men, add more boulders to the pile. Perhaps the next round will get one of them to speak." The judge then shifted his eyes back to Mrs. Corey. He watched with glee her appalled reaction to his command as she fell to the ground.

The guards rolled several boulders to the wagon from behind one of the buildings near the town square. After an hour, a pile of stones sat at the end of the wagon. The crowd watched the humiliating torture as the smaller stones we added to the heap. Giles Corey groaning in agony with each placement. The guards gathered at the end to lift the sixth stone. It required three men to lift it from the ground and another set of three men to walk the few steps with the stone to the wagon's edge. Several more guards jumped up to help. Four men standing on the wagon lifted the weight, shuffling to stand over Mr. Giles Corey, ready to stack the rock onto the already heavy burden blanketing the old man. One guard slipped, losing his grip. The other guards panicked and dropped the remaining weight quickly, losing their balance, and all fell over the wagon.

The roars and screams of the crowd echoed off nearby buildings as the guards got back on their feet. Shrieks and cries filled the area. The guards, first confused, turned to look at Mr. Corey. A couple stumbled back again at the horrific scene. Blood gurgled from Giles Corey's mouth as, still alive, he grappled for breath. Rock appeared on the wagon where the old man's stomach should be. The boulders flattened his body to a fraction of an inch.

As the citizens whispered in ever-increasing tones, the onlookers turned their attention to the orchestrator of the torture. Judgment showed in every eye cast in his direction—the punishment far outweighed any ill-proven crime. The wailing of Mrs. Corey's sobs drummed the crowd's discord into a fever pitch. The judge raised his hands as the crowd turned still.

Moments ticked by without a sound, then a bloodcurdling crunch followed by Mr. Corey's final breath fell upon everyone's ears.

Townies roared with a change of heart and began throwing rocks, food, and other items at the podium. The guards panicked and didn't know which direction to focus their attention.

Once the first projectile landed near the judge's spot on the stand, he scurried off the podium. A few steps from the bottom, he squatted down next to Cristiane, exposing jagged teeth through a hideous smile. "Take note, Carolyn. Your turn is fast approaching." He paused and waited for her reaction. Under his breath, he laughed to himself. Pleased with her horror-stricken shock, he slapped her on the shoulder as he continued away from the mayhem.

Barely a moment passed, and Cristiane's anger boiled up inside her. "You're deranged! What kind of sick, vile person are you? I am not Carolyn. I am not Carol—"

She heard incessant banging on her door, which bolted her upright, startled and confused, until her head cleared from the dream.

"Crissy, Crissy! What is going on? Are you alright?" Jeffrey Bradford banged on his daughter's bedroom door. "Why is the door locked?"

"Dad, I'm okay. Nothing to worry about." Cristiane rubbed the sleep from her eyes, got out of bed, and opened the door.

"That was scary. Are you sure you're alright, sweetie? You were screaming." Jeffrey put a hand on Cristiane's head and smoothed the hair from her eyes while her mom looked on from the hall. He put the back of his hand on her forehead. "You're sweating. Are you ill?"

She brushed her dad's hand away, annoyed by the dream and their intrusion. "Dad, I'm fine. It's nothing. A weird dream, that's all. I had a bunch of pillows and covers over me."

"Why's the door locked?" Her mother, Beatrice, darted eyes around the room.

Cristiane gave her mother a look as she answered. "Seriously, Mom? You and Dad were still out when I got to bed. Look under the bed and in the closet if it makes you feel better." Cristiane withdrew from the door, dramatic, swinging her arms around the bedroom. "Have a good look. David's not here. He didn't even go to the party."

Her mother walked around the room for a few seconds while Jeffrey stood at the door. "What do you mean—David didn't go? Did you break up?" Beatrice stopped and tilted her head, full of curiosity. Her arms folded, looking at her daughter while she waited for an answer.

"No, Mom. We didn't break up." Cristiane, exasperated and rolling her eyes, put her hand on the door, ushering her parents out. "Can we talk about this in the daylight? I'd like to get some sleep."

"Of course, Sweetie. Glad you're okay. Bea, let's all get some sleep." Jeffrey beckoned from the door.

Monday Morning

Cristiane walked into AP Chemistry in a much better mood. She thought back on the events of the weekend, and although Robby confirmed the ghost sightings, she did not let it get to her. The odd dream felt real at the time, but quickly left her mind after dealing with her parents in the middle of the night. Their meddlesome questions the following morning had her making a quick exit to see David at the hospital.

However, the necklace weighed heavily on her. She had not been able to remove it since David first put it around her neck. After school, she would try cutting the chain if David could not undo the clasp for her. Cris didn't want to bother him about it yesterday, as he was going home.

Cristiane spent most of Sunday with David, waiting for him to get approval to leave the hospital and then going home with David and his parents. She helped get him set up in the ground-floor guest room, so he would not have to climb the stairs while his broken leg healed. With his dad's help, they moved his desk and set up his computer, and then she finished with gathered clothes and putting them in the guest room dresser.

This morning, she walked him to his first-period class before heading to AP Chem.

As she sat down, Mr. Patten stopped at her table. He was a few years older than his students and flirted with several of the girls. It was a surprise to all that the principal had not fired him yet because of his behavior. If he had crossed the line with any of the students, no one was complaining.

"Good morning, Cristiane. Did you have a good weekend? You had a birthday, didn't you? Eighteen, right?" He asked as he placed his hand on her shoulder.

Cristiane moved back from his touch. "Sure, Mr. Patten. My birthday was Saturday. Yes. I'm eighteen now. Besides David's car accident, the weekend was all right."

"Oh good, good. Happy birthday, by the way! Eighteen huh... Well, that makes you legal now, doesn't it?" He watched if his question sparked a response. When Cristiane didn't reply. "You are going to register to vote soon, aren't you?"

"Of course, as soon as I can." Cristiane opened her bag and took out her notebook, ignoring the fact that Mr. Patten was still regarding her. After a moment, he walked to his desk and busied himself with the day's lesson plan.

Jessica sat down next to her at the lab table. "What was all that about?"

"Good question. He knows it was my eighteenth birthday. Mr. Patten is good-looking, but what an odd teacher. Some days, he creeps me out." Cristiane finished pulling out the supplies for class and set her bag on the floor.

"Oh, I know." Jessica nodded to Cristiane as her eyes remained locked on their teacher. The way Jessica looked at Mr. Patten made Cristiane think she would not complain if he made some advances her way. However, Jessica was still seventeen. One thing Cristiane knew, Mr. Patten didn't flirt with the underage girls. He had scruples, at least to a degree.

Throughout the lesson, Mr. Patten used Jessica and Cristiane's table as his area to illustrate what he expected from the day's lab. Cristiane tried to ignore his attempts to touch her hand as he picked up a slide or placed one back on the table. At the end of his demonstration, he made a point of taking Cristiane's hand while guiding the class in wishing her a belated happy birthday.

Blushing, Cristiane tried to pull her hand away from Mr. Patten as he lightly stroked the top of her hand while students sang to her. The attention mortified her, as she watched around the room at her classmates, each singing and enjoying the razzing. As the class finished the last line, he released his grasp.

"That was great, class. Happy birthday, Cristiane." He put his hand on her shoulder again and immediately pulled it away. "Wow!" He looked down while walking back to his desk. Cristiane could see that his hand was red and blistered. She realized that she was also shivering.

What the hell is going on? She wondered as she looked hesitantly around the room. Obviously, none of her fellow students noticed a temperature change. Jessica started the lab and was looking into the microscope. That freed Cristiane to look around the room. She locked eyes with Mr. Patten. He was wrapping his hand with gauze and looking at Cristiane with confusion.

Cristiane quickly looked away. In her mind, she was working out the events of the past few days. Since she started wearing the necklace, every guy that touched her—David, Jack, and now Mr. Patten—had been injured. Did the necklace or ghost have something to do with it? She continued to half-heartedly do the lab assignment. Instead of focusing on classwork, her thoughts lingered over David's accident, Jack's pool incident, and now Mr. Patten's hand.

Cristiane worked alongside Jessica to finish before the end of class, but Jess was doing most of the work. Cristiane gave an apology and swore to return the favor, feeling guilty for not doing her share.

"No worries. I know you're worried about David after his accident," Jessica responded as she finished up their lab report and turned it in as the bell rang.

Robby walked up behind Cristiane in the hallway after class. "Hey, we have to meet tonight and talk about what happened this weekend." He took her arm and turned her to face him. He lowered his voice as he looked up and down the hall. "I talked with someone, someone that knows about this stuff. When I told her you thought you might be related to the women in the crypt, she said it was important for you two to meet soon."

"Wow! What more did she say?" Cristiane was intrigued, yet hesitant.

"Nothing. I've talked with her before about things I have seen. Most people in town think she's a quack, but she knows what she's talking about with spirits, witchcraft, you know, *unusual* stuff." Robby looked down as they walked to their next class. "I've seen ghosts and heard voices, things like that since I can remember. I told Tina once, and she flipped, so I've never mentioned it to her again." Robby shrugged. "Kind of funny too, since her grandmother's spirit likes to hang around a lot to make sure she's okay. Her grandma likes to get in the way, if you know what I mean. Tina wants to move things along, but her grandma shows up and starts giving me a tough time, whispering in my ear to back off and stuff. It's annoying."

Cristiane slapped him on the shoulder. "Ah, so that's it. Tina was wondering why you weren't making any moves. Should I tell her why?" She gave Robby a playful shove as they stopped in front of his next class.

"All right, where do I meet you and when?"

"I'll send you a text with the address. I can't make it until after work, so around eight o'clock, okay?"

Robby turned as Cristiane walked down the hall.

"Great! See ya later," Cristiane called, already down by her class door.

Monday Night

The address Robby gave her was on the outskirts of town, in a slightly run-down area. It wasn't tent-city, but it was not shiny and new like Cristiane's neighborhood. She started to step out of the car and then hesitated; Robby wasn't there yet. She didn't want to stand outside. The neighbors might think she was loitering around the lady's house. Cristiane instinctively locked the doors, turned up the music, and waited.

As she dozed off, freezing air filled the car. Cristiane's eyes fluttered under heavy lids while she shivered with the sudden temperature drop. A dull blue light hovered over the passenger's seat. Or was it light across the street? Quickly sitting up straighter, she rubbed the sleep from her eyes. The light was definitely in her car. Not trusting what she saw, she blinked again while extending her hand slowly toward the sphere. Her breath was visible as she breathed out; it seemed to hit a tall figure and then disperse.

A loud tapping caused her to jump in her seat. Turning, she saw it was Robby, then quickly twisting back to look at the passenger seat—the light was gone.

As she got out of her car, Robby stepped back to clear her way. "Jumpy tonight, huh?"

"Did you see that light in my car?"

Robby bent down to see what she was talking about. "What light?"

"Oh, forget it. Well, it isn't every day you go to a psychic, or whatever, to rid yourself of ghosts. Now I'm having weird dreams, seeing strange lights, and I can't get this necklace off, either." Cristiane tugged at it to emphasize her point as they walked toward the house. "I saw David a while ago and told him. He tried to get it off, too. He said the clasp looked like it was fused together or something. I even tried bolt cutters. Nothing works."

"If anyone can fix what's going on with you, Isadora is the lady. I wouldn't know what else to do about your umm—situation." Robby pressed the doorbell as an older woman opened the door, causing Cristiane to jump back. "Wow, still touchy, I see!"

"Good evening, Robby," Isadora greeted. However, her gaze was on Cristiane and the necklace. She raised her hand to Cristiane's neck, stopping an inch or so from the pendant. "Ah, yes. There is great power radiating from this talisman."

Cristiane's eyes were glued to the old woman's thin, wrinkled hand below her chin. Isadora was the oldest-looking person Cristiane had ever seen. She could not help but look the woman over from head to toe. Her hair was white as snow, disheveled and wavy, as long layers cascaded down her hunched, narrow shoulders. She wore a dress that appeared five sizes too big, swallowing the old lady up in the fabric, making her appear even smaller. Her skin was blotchy and bruised in some areas. As elderly skin is tender, it was apparent that she needed to take much care to prevent injury. Translucent in appearance, her pale skin reminded Cristiane of the ghosts she wanted to escape. She looked at Isadora's face. The woman had the lightest, clear blue eyes and they pierced Cristiane's gaze. She was ready to get started with the evening's meeting.

"We have a great deal to go over Cristiane, descendent of Rachel." Isadora noticed the jaw-dropping surprise on Cristiane and Robby as she ushered them inside. "Don't be alarmed, it is true. Still, this is not something to fear but to embrace. Once, of course, we take care of that pendant."

Isadora was the last to enter. She took a handful of smoldering twigs tied together and carried it back to the open door. She brushed the air with the smoke. A hint of lavender filled Cristiane's nostrils as the fumes lightly filled the air. Isadora finished her ritual and put the twig bundle back in a nearby container. She closed the heavy doors after whispering a quick chant.

"Here, sit around the table, please. I will tell you the history I know before I tell you what we must do tomorrow night." Isadora sat at the small round table after lighting several candles around the tiny room.

Cristiane and Robby looked at each other, both afraid to speak.

"Cristiane, confirm your full name before we begin. Help yourself to the cookies on the table. If you'd like something other than tea or soda, ask. Shall we start?" Isadora waited for them to pick a treat and drink. As the teens settled back into their seats, a nod from both ensured they were ready. Once Cristiane acknowledged her full name, Isadora began with the history of North Andover.

"North Andover has a long and controversial history. Our modest New Hampshire town was once simply called Andover. Several generations ago, many people were accused of witchcraft here. As we are so close to Salem, they escorted many accused to Salem for trial and further punishment, even execution. Most were sent home, as Salem's trials had nothing to do with witches and much more to do with government oppression. Fear, by people in power, of what they did not understand—whether that be mental illness, assertiveness, or the growing distrust of the local government—all fueled the tumultuous times. A war on witches fed the hysteria—whether the accused were actual witches was irrelevant.

"However, a few Andover residents never went to trial and suffered a horrible death by the townspeople. Rachel Madison's mother, Carolyn, and aunt were among them. At the height of the witch hunts and trials in Andover and Salem Village, they hung Carolyn in the town square in 1692. There was no tangible evidence against her mother. The shenanigans of a few townspeople, wild accusations without evidence, likely thinking it was sport to stir up so much controversy.

"Rachel's Aunt Prudence moved into seclusion after her sister's death. There were rumors she worked on potions and spells in her modest cottage on the outskirts of town. Nonetheless, after the hysteria over the trials and thoughts that so many innocent women died, the people of Andover left her alone for a brief time. She had a reputation as a quirky aging woman, forever damaged by the death of her sister.

"Rachel, however, lived with Prudence after her mother's death, as her father passed away when Rachel was around two or three years old. Rachel knew firsthand Prudence's abilities with magic and witchcraft. A young lady herself, Rachel was expected to marry in a couple of years and free her aunt from the burden of raising her. As both her parents were gone, Rachel dropped the last name Brown to distance herself from her mother's history and tragic demise.

"Still, the family legend tells of Rachel becoming quite promiscuous after her mother's death and cavorting with young men in town. Her aunt branded Rachel a harlot and adulterer. As the story has passed down through the ages, Prudence put a spell on that very necklace you have on your neck, required her young niece to always wear it. Any man that touched Rachel became violently ill.

"A few weeks later, Prudence was the subject of a local mob's desire to rid the town of her oddity and witchcraft. They tied Prudence up on a pole with her hands behind her back in the middle of town. The men nailed in a short block so she could rest her feet, but it served to prolong her torture. Angry with Prudence, Rachel was the only witness and would not come to her aunt's defense. Local authorities, even the influential judge, ignored what the townspeople were doing to Prudence.

"Prudence didn't help herself, either. She refused to confess and spent several days strung up in the middle of town without food. Water was sparingly offered until it was plain that she would not incriminate herself, so that too was taken away. The townspeople found Prudence guilty, without a formal trial, and burned her at the stake in an open bonfire. The citizens watched without offering her aid, listening to her screams until the flames scorched her lungs and she could no longer scream or breathe. Rachel did not attend the execution.

"With nowhere else to go, Rachel took up residence in her aunt's house and lived there until her death. Some say she married a soldier after her aunt's death, although he was not seen by anyone in town. Others say she never married and was pregnant before Prudence was killed.

"Rachel gave birth to a baby girl a few months after her aunt's death. Obviously, Prudence's attempts to keep men away from her niece were too late. Rachel's daughter grew up to be quite beautiful and married a prominent doctor in the community. The woman you know from the grave marker to be Constance Madison Worthington.

"Rachel always wore the necklace. The town residents thought she wore it because she felt guilty for not speaking up on behalf of her aunt, guilty then for sentencing her to death. However, another legend claims that the necklace was cursed, and that Rachel could not remove it without causing harm to herself. The necklace remained on her neck for burial at the insistence of her daughter, who stated Rachel never took it off for fear of a sudden violent death."

Cristiane touched the necklace around her neck. "Is that why I can't remove it now? It is cursed?" Fear was evident in her shaking voice.

"Yes, dear. I am afraid that is precisely why it cannot be removed. We must perform a few rituals tomorrow night, All Hallows' Eve. Not only to remove the curse on the pendant, but to help Rachel and Prudence be free and move on in the realm where they belong. Their spirits have been trapped for centuries with that pendant in the crypt. It is quite a miracle that you were the one to wear it. I believe the power of a family witch is the only component that was able to free them from bondage."

"I am not a witch," Cristiane protested. She looked to Robby for support but found none. He only shrugged and shook his head in acceptance. Quietly, she repeated, "I am not a witch."

"Ah, but you are, young lady. And a mighty powerful one with a long family legacy. Although almost all of those prosecuted in Salem and Andover centuries ago were simple folks trying to make a life in the new world, a handful were actual witches. Your ancestors being among them. What I sense, anyone other than a mighty witch cannot wield the energy emitting from that pendant. I will know more after the rituals are over. First, we must help your ancestors resolve their dilemma and cross over."

"But why is this pendant so special? Is there significance to the shape of the emerald stones? The pendant is—odd." Cristiane had regained her voice, although her hands were shaking. She knotted her fingers together to quell their movement and peered back at Isadora for an answer.

"It is like a rune, found in pagan worship and witchcraft. See the strange shapes of the emeralds creating a triangle? It is actually a triquetra surrounded by the Celtic design in pewter. The triquetra has many meanings, but for witches, it is a symbol of protection. Furthermore, it symbolizes the Wiccan triple goddess, and the integrated parts of our existence, referring to mind, body, and soul. It is an immensely powerful symbol. Combining the emeralds with the powers of a triquetra, among other elements, and then the addition of a powerful spell means that piece carries a heavy burden. I do not dare touch the pendant. Could you turn it over for me, Cristiane?" Isadora asked.

A look of adoration crossed Isadora's face. Her eyes sparkling. "Oh, this is a well-crafted talisman." She reached over and grabbed a table mirror so Cristiane could see what was on the backside. "See the two facing crescent moons? Each moon phase has meaning; the waning and waxing moons are meant to cast out troubles and start fresh. Wait. There is something underneath. Cristiane, try to pull the moons apart if you can."

Cristiane started to touch the moons when an apparition appeared, hovering above the table. While Robby fell back in his chair, Cristiane screamed. Isadora was the only one to remain calm as a smile lit up her face.

Isadora waited patiently for Robby to right himself in the chair. "Prudence, would you be so kind as to open the talisman? We would like to admire your handiwork." Isadora leaned slightly toward Cristiane and nodded as she placed a hand on her shoulder. "It's all right. Prudence is proud of her work and will open it for us. Don't be frightened."

"Has sh—she been here the whole time?" Cristiane's voice trembled and her hand wavered as she pointed at Prudence.

"Well, of course. Rachel and Prudence have been by your side since you put on that necklace. I assume Prudence has been acting as a bit of unwanted protection." With that comment, the floating figure turned to Isadora.

"Prudence, you have been interfering." Isadora's tone was that of a respected school teacher. "Rachel has been trying to protect the people in your path. Both you and Rachel need to move on and leave poor Cristiane alone."

Prudence hovered within inches of Isadora's face. Her smoky image swayed back and forth for a moment, and then straightened up. She looked at each person around the table and nodded at Isadora. The apparition turned toward Cristiane and leaned in close, within inches of her face. A wispy hand caressed along Cristiane's eyebrow and down to her chin, then slightly lifted her hair. Cristiane touched her own cheek. "Oh! Oh my, I feel her. She—she seems kindhearted and maybe—I don't know, lonely. I can feel that. Sense it in my soul. Is that strange?"

Prudence seemed to droop and lowered her head. A few seconds passed, then tenderly, Prudence opened the back of the pendant and vanished from sight.

"Well, I don't think she enjoyed hearing that lonely bit, but she is ready to leave us. That is a good sign. So, let's see what is inside. Oh my, she has opened two compartments."

Behind the moons was an etched pentagram with the initials P. M. centered under the star. The circular piece of pewter was opened again, revealing that it was also a locket. Cristiane pulled the locket open further to reveal the contents. Tucked inside was an embroidered piece of lace with an M monogrammed in the center holding a lock of curled hair.

Isadora took a small, lidded container and passed it to Cristiane. "Take the hair and place it in here. I am sure that is a lock of Rachel's hair when she was a baby. The lace more than likely belonged to Carolyn, Rachel's mother. No wonder Prudence was trapped with Rachel and the pendant. There is a great family bond connecting their souls to this jewel."

"Isadora, how are we going to help Cristiane? This is all remarkably interesting and intriguing, but what can we do about it?" Robby had not spoken since they sat down. Now he was ready to do something about everything they had learned tonight.

"Yes, Robby. You are right. It is time to move on for all of us." Isadora busied herself with cleaning up the table. "Tomorrow night, we must meet at the crypt where their remains are enshrined. Do you have two friends you trust with this information?"

Cristiane and Robby glanced at each other. Robby knew they had a couple of friends to assist. "Yes, we can have David, Cristiane's boyfriend, come with us. My girlfriend Tina can come as well. She doesn't believe in ghosts or any of this. Perhaps the gathering will help her realize what I've been seeing and hearing all my life."

Both Cristiane and Isadora laughed at Robby. "Well, that's one way to introduce her to the craft and prove spirits exist." Isadora rose, took the tray back to the kitchen, and then came back to the others. "We must have them join us, as we need five people for the ritual, one for each point of the pentagram. Let's meet at ten o'clock tomorrow night and do not bring anyone else."

With that said, Cristiane and Robby got up from the table and bid Isadora good night.

All Hallows' Eve

Isadora, David, and Cristiane were putting the last touches on the ritual necessities when they heard Tina and Robby approach.

"Robby, none of this makes any sense. You're talking crazy again. Stop trying to scare me. It's not gonna work." Tina obviously wasn't buying what Robby mentioned about the ceremony. She stopped at the opening to the crypt, noticing the preparations. "So, you three are in on this, too? How crazy are we trying to make our last Halloween together, anyway?"

Tina entered and walked around slowly. She looked over the candles, the pentagram marked on the floor, the water container, sacks of herbs, and oils. "This is a bit much for the charade, don't ya think?"

Isadora spoke. "My dear, this is not a charade. We gathered to help remove the curse that has passed to your friend. As we succeed in that task, we also free the spirits that are trapped in this reality. The veil between the living and the dead is thinnest on All Hallows' Eve. Tonight is the best chance we have to guide Rachel and Prudence to their rightful place. We need your help to do that. Are you willing to stand here and do as I ask, so we can be successful on both fronts?"

Isadora stood close to Tina, took her hands, and gazed into her eyes. She was patient, letting Tina know she was indeed serious. After a moment, considering each person, Tina looked back at Isadora and nodded.

"Good." Isadora squeezed Tina's hands and nodding her thanks. "Then let us begin. Each of you, please put on one of the black robes and stand at a tip of the pentagram. Be careful not to topple the containers at your feet. We have several banishing spell concoctions within this small space to deal with the multiple layers of power within the emerald pendant and assist Rachel and Prudence toward their proper place. At your feet are small bowls filled with charcoal topped with banishing herbs. I will light those shortly.

"Turn your attention to the center. On top of Rachel's sarcophagus, I have placed a container of rainwater. The natural elements in the rainwater work to absorb the negative energy expelled once we succeed in lifting the curse. We will dispose of the rainwater properly when we are done. Next, I have candles infused with a blend of banishing oil, cloves, garlic, and basil. The candles are crucial as they help exorcise the bond Prudence and Rachel have to the pendant. Once the connection is broken, their souls will be lifted and free to depart from this dimension. I will give each of you a stone. Keep this stone in your left hand, even as we hold hands. Our connected energies go through the stones—through all of us, like a circuit. The energy builds up to light the way for Prudence and Rachel on their journey to the afterlife. As we chant and meditate, we strengthen the banishing spell and give it the power to help Rachel and Prudence move on."

Isadora handed each of them a stone. The stones were smooth and marked with Latin characters and other intriguing markings. "Repeat this chant as I light the torches at your feet and the candles surrounding us."

> Spirits of Protection,
> Spirits who clear
> Eliminate all phantoms
> Who don't belong here!

Cristiane looked at the stone in her left hand, then nodded to David as she stretched out her arm to take his hand. She began the chant as the others joined hands, one after the other. David continued by taking Tina's hand and Tina to Robby. As the foursome began to synchronize the chanting, Isadora joined the group between Robby and Cristiane.

Isadora pulled from her cloak pocket the tiny bit of lace and hair she retrieved from the locket and placed them over the flame at her feet. Dark smoke crackled and hissed as the items burned, then fell to the ground within the circle. The trail of smoke moved up, but remained within the confines of the group. As Cristiane wrapped her hand around Isadora's, a jolt of electricity sent a shiver through her body as the circle was complete. As she looked at her friends, she noticed each had a similar experience.

"Close your eyes. Continue the chant and meditate on what we want to accomplish. We must free the pendant of the curse and the bond that has held Rachel's and Prudence's spirits to this place." Isadora looked at each thoughtfully, waiting for each to close their eyes as requested.

Several minutes traveled by as the group chanted the mantra. Cristiane felt a warmth channel through her, starting at her core and working out to her hands. As the gathering continued the ritual, she felt the pendant warm at her neck. She stole a peek and noticed the smoke from the burned items was now a tight stream rapidly moving within the confines made by their hands. It stopped and hovered for a few seconds as if it noticed Cristiane was watching. Then bolted toward Cristiane and struck her along the collarbone.

"Ouch!" Cristiane tried to pull her hand away from Isadora.

"Don't break the circle!" Isadora held firmly to Cristiane's hand. "Whatever happens, do not break the circle."

Cristiane relaxed and nodded in agreement. She looked down, continuing the chant with the others. The emeralds were glowing deep in their cores as if they were lit from the inside. With each chant, the light grew brighter and brighter. Suddenly, a beam of light poured from the pendant's center and shot through the crypt. Just as quickly, the necklace fell from Cristiane's neck to the floor.

Isadora turned to Cristiane. "Good! Keep chanting. The curse is broken. Now let us help Cristiane's family cross over." Isadora closed her eyes again and squeezed Cristiane's hand, indicating she should do the same.

Realizing the ritual was indeed working, each chanted with more conviction. The energy was palpable in the small chamber as the crescendo grew louder and louder. A breeze began to swirl within the group, and the wind stirred stronger and faster. The air cooled to where goosebumps appearing on their flesh. With a whirl of protest, Prudence appeared in the middle of the gathering, facing Cristiane.

"My wonderful young niece, you have a fantastic force lying dormant within you. Learn how to channel your magical abilities, and one day you will make a fine witch." Prudence intoned through the chamber as she hovered stoically above the tomb.

A moment later, Rachel appeared as well. "Thank you, Cristiane, for freeing us. Without your help, we would have been doomed to this tiny chamber for eternity. You are brave and show great strength beyond that of many witches. Keep the emerald pendant with you, as one day its energy may be of use to you. You have broken the family curse. It's no longer a threat to you, but a power source when required. You control the qualities within it now—

use them wisely." Rachel's translucent shape picked up the pendant. Rachel took Cristiane's right hand and placed the jewel in her palm, closing Cristiane's fingers around it.

As the circle broke, a final gust of wind swirled through the chamber. Rachel and Prudence regarded Isadora with a last nod of thanks and admiration. They acknowledged Isadora's skill and craft at mastering the ritual and freeing them of captivity. Their forms drifted out of sight as the wind blew out each candle, and an eerie fog gathered above the water basin in the center. Slowly, the mist lowered into rainwater as if being pulled into submission until the onlookers saw nothing more than clear water.

"Splendid, everyone! That was quite splendid!" Isadora congratulated her new circle of young friends as the group cheered their success. "Cristiane, please help me with the basin while the others pick up the other items."

After Isadora and Cristiane dumped the water in a hole far away from the crypt and then covered it with earth, Isadora took Cristiane by the hands and smiled. "Did you take to heart what Rachel and Prudence said in there?"

Cristiane appeared confused for a moment.

Isadora tilted her head, scrunching her eyes at Cristiane. "My dear, *you* most certainly are a witch. What you do with the information is up to you."

Cristiane started to protest, then thought better of it and remained quiet, taking in all that transpired throughout the evening. Her collarbone began to ache, reminding her of the dagger of smoke that came at her during the ceremony. She raised her hand to feel the damage.

Isadora fished for something inside her robe. Lightly, she touched Cristiane's collarbone with a handkerchief, where a long gash along the bone trickled blood. "It could have been worse." She took Cristiane's hands in her own, and then, with a broad smile and a final, firm squeeze of her hands. "I'll be here to help when you are ready."

She left Cristiane standing in the middle of the cemetery as she turned back toward the crypt.

Cristiane fished the pendant out of a pocket. She felt a purpose unlike anything she felt before as it sparkled in the moonlight, and she turned it over and over in her hand. *Is my life going to change? Can I go to college? I have so many questions.*

While she looked up at the moonlight sky, wondering what this new revelation meant for her future, her friends came running out to greet her.

"I always knew you were wicked, Cris, but a witch. I'm so excited, babe." David scooped his arms around her, cuddling into her neck.

"Don't get too excited, big guy," Cristiane matched his embrace. "I'm happy to have a few answers, but I have so many new questions."

"Yes, but you have all of us by your side," Robby confirmed. "Even Tina is coming around. Isn't that right, sweetie?"

"I must admit, it's disturbing, but I can't deny what I saw tonight. Of course, I'm in." Tina put her arm around Robby and gave him a quick kiss. "We're with you, Cris. No matter what."

"Thanks, guys," Cristiane pulled back as the others caught up. "I'm not nearly as freaked out in the cemetery as I was last week. But I get the feeling this is only the beginning." She turned toward their cars, ready to leave as the others followed her.

David stayed by her side and jested, "Can we test out your powers with a lottery win or something?"

"Oh, that's a great idea, David." The guys gave each other a fist bump.

Cristiane laughed and shuddered her head. "Or something. I have no idea how to do anything or if I'll be any good at casting." Cristiane stopped a few feet from her car and pointed toward it. "Do you see that? Anyone? Look in my car."

"What? I see nothing. Robby, what about you?" David turned to the other couple.

"The orb? Yep, I see it, Cris," Robby stopped alongside the others and bent down for a better view.

"It was in my car last night as I waited for Robby before we saw Isadora, too. I dismissed it since I was half asleep." Cristiane slowly ventured closer, with Robby right behind her. "It's here again, so it's not Rachel or Prudence. What does it mean?"

Robby leaned in closer, and it quickly disappeared. "I don't think we're going to find an answer tonight. At least an orb can't hurt you. Mention it to Isadora when you speak to her next. Don't worry about it; you're safe. I've seen dozens of orbs, but none in my own car." Robby stood up and turned back to his friends with a toothy grin. "Looks like the adventures are going to start sooner than you thought."

"Yay, me." Cristiane raised a fist in a nervous gesture. "I wonder how many more apparitions will seek me out?"

They exchanged hugs and filed into their cars. The modest caravan crept through the graveyard on All Hallows' Eve toward the exit. They went by a few cars that drove into the cemetery with teens dressed in costume, shouting boos and hisses into the night air, laughing and having fun. Cristiane kept an eye on the cars as she passed by them, creeping the car in the direction of the exit. Looking through her rearview mirror, the newcomers were heading into the area she and her friends had left.

In her corner view, she saw the orb again as it hovered in her backseat above the headrest. *What are you and what do you want with me?*

Epilogue

"Isadora, you should have consulted me prior to the ceremony with such a candidate."

Her leader's words dumbfounded Isadora. Shocked, she looked at each member of her coven. Stone-faced, none showed a hint of sorrow or concern. "Why would I need to do such a thing? You have not questioned the intentions of a coven sponsorship in the past. What could make you question Cristiane's intentions?"

Cristiane heard her name and stood to listen more closely to the exchange between Isadora and the High Priestess.

"She is the daughter of Beatrice, isn't she?" High Priestess Sarah folded her arms across her chest. She did not expect to have an issue with the initiation ceremony, becoming increasingly irritated with the direction the evening was headed.

"Well, yes. Beatrice is her mother's name, but she isn't a practicing witch. I have guided Cristiane's training. Beatrice is not involved with this." Isadora fought to control her trembling lip and rise to her voice. She continued after taking a cleansing breath. "How do you, High Priestess, know Beatrice Bradford? Why would Cristiane's mother give you pause?"

"I'm sorry, Isadora. I cannot welcome your inductee this evening. Her mother is a highly active witch. If her daughter is unaware, then I suggest you both tread with caution. Carefully investigate why Beatrice has not disclosed or shared her practice with her daughter."

Cristiane stood in stunned silence. Her eyes were shining in the moonlight as she held back tears. She covered her mouth with her hands, reminding herself not to scream a retort or interrupt to ask her own questions. Her mind raced as she tried to recall a moment when she might have questioned her mother's actions or noticed a bit of casting, especially in the past two years. Nothing. *Has mom lied to me all these years?*

"Tread carefully, Isadora. As you know, we are a modern coven, promoting individual enlightenment and holistic practices. Beatrice chose a contentious path—a dark, sinister path. Until I am confident her mother's direction does not influence Cristiane, she is not welcome to join our coven."

About the Author

SIRRAH MEDEIROS is a writer, editor, and occasional poet. She is the author of several published horror short stories included in various anthologies and the author of a self-published poetry collection, *Seasons of Sentiment: A Collection of Poetry and Prose* (2014). Sirrah devoted much of her life moving and traveling around the world while an active-duty Marine, and then later as a Marine Corps spouse serving in support of local unit families. She spent a sizable portion of her career as a technical communicator and program manager and now spends her time creating artwork, writing and editing fiction while enjoying a wonderful life pursuing her passions. Sirrah lives in Northern Virginia with her family and two playful dogs.

You can find her on Facebook, Instagram, Amazon, Goodreads, and Twitter.

Thank you for reading. If you enjoyed this story, we hope you'll leave a review and continue to follow Sirrah Medeiros as the Cristiane Bradford series unfolds, as well as discover her other upcoming releases at https://sirrahmedeiros.com.

www.ingramcontent.com/pod-product-compliance
Lightning Source LLC
Chambersburg PA
CBHW031018041025
33464CB00009B/406